Tawny Scrawny Lion

by **Kathryn Jackson** • illustrated by **Gustaf Tenggren**

A GOLDEN BOOK • NEW YORK

Golden Books Publishing Company, Inc., New York, New York 10106

Once there was a tawny, scrawny, hungry lion who never could get enough to eat.

He chased monkeys on Monday—

kangaroos on Tuesday—

zebras on Wednesday—

bears on Thursday—

camels on Friday—

and on Saturday, elephants!

And since he caught everything he ran after, that lion should have been as fat as butter. But he wasn't at all. The more he ate, the scrawnier and hungrier he grew.

The other animals didn't feel one bit safe. They stood at a distance and tried to talk things over with the tawny, scrawny lion.

"It's all your fault for running away," he grumbled. "If I didn't have to run, run, run for every single bite I get, I'd be fat as butter and

sleek as satin. Then I wouldn't have to eat so much, and you'd last longer!"

Just then, a fat little rabbit came hopping through the forest, picking berries. All the big animals looked at him and grinned slyly.

"Rabbit," they said. "Oh, you lucky rabbit! We appoint you to talk things over with the lion."

That made the little rabbit feel very proud.
"What shall I talk about?" he asked eagerly.
"Any old thing," said the big animals. "The
important thing is to go right up close."
So the fat little rabbit hopped right up to the
big hungry lion and counted his ribs.

"You look much too scrawny to talk things over," he said. "So how about supper at my house first?"

"What's for supper?" asked the lion.

The little rabbit said, "Carrot stew." That sounded awful to the lion. But the little rabbit said, "Yes sir, my five fat sisters and my four fat

brothers are making a delicious big carrot stew right now!"

"What are we waiting for?" cried the lion. And he went hopping away with the little rabbit, thinking of ten fat rabbits, and looking just as jolly as you please.

"Well," grinned all the big animals. "That should take care of Tawny-Scrawny for today."

Before very long, the lion began to wonder if they would ever get to the rabbit's house.

First, the fat little rabbit kept stopping to pick berries and mushrooms and all sorts of good-smelling herbs. And when his basket was full, what did he do but flop down on the river bank!

"Wait a bit," he said.

"I want to catch a few fish for the stew."

That was almost too much for the hungry lion.

For a moment, he thought he would have to eat that one little rabbit then and there. But he kept saying, "five fat sisters and four fat brothers" over and over to himself. And at last the two were on their way again.

"Here we are!" said the rabbit, hopping around a turn with the lion close behind him. Sure enough, there was the rabbit's house, with a big pot of carrot stew bubbling over an open fire.

And sure enough, there were nine more fat, merry little rabbits hopping around it!

When they saw the fish, they popped them into the stew, along with the mushrooms and herbs. The stew began to smell very good indeed.

And when they saw the tawny, scrawny lion, they gave him a big bowl of hot stew. And then they hopped about so busily, that really, it would have been quite a job for that tired,

hungry lion to catch even one of them!

So he gobbled his stew, but the rabbits filled his bowl again. When he had eaten all he could hold, they heaped his bowl with berries.

And when the berries were gone—the tawny, scrawny lion wasn't scrawny any more! He felt so good and fat and comfortable that he couldn't even move.

"Here's a fine thing!" he said to himself. "All these fat little rabbits, and I haven't room inside for even one!"

He looked at all those fine, fat little rabbits and wished he'd get hungry again.

"Mind if I stay a while?" he asked.

"We wouldn't even hear of your going!" said the rabbits. Then they plumped themselves down in the lion's lap and began to sing songs.

And somehow, even when it was time to say goodnight, that lion wasn't one bit hungry!

Home he went, through the soft moonlight, singing softly to himself. He curled up in his bed, patted his sleek, fat tummy, and smiled.

When he woke up in the morning, it was Monday.

"Time to chase monkeys!" said the lion.

But he wasn't one bit hungry for monkeys! What he wanted was some more of that tasty carrot stew. So off he went to visit the rabbits.

On Tuesday he didn't want kangaroos, and on Wednesday he didn't want zebras. He wasn't hungry for bears on Thursday, or camels on Friday, or elephants on Saturday.

All the big animals were so surprised and happy!
They dressed in their best and went to see the fat little rabbit.

"Rabbit," they said. "Oh, you wonderful rabbit! What in the world did you talk to the tawny, scrawny, hungry, terrible lion about?"

The fat little rabbit jumped up in the air and said, "Oh, my goodness! We had such a good time with that nice, jolly lion that I guess we forgot to talk about anything at all!"

And before the big animals could say one word, the tawny lion came skipping up the path. He had a basket of berries for the fat rabbit sisters, and a string of fish for the fat rabbit brothers, and a big bunch of daisies for the fat rabbit himself.

"I came for supper," he said, shaking paws all around.

Then he sat down in the soft grass, looking fat as butter, sleek as satin, and jolly as all get out, all ready for another good big supper of carrot stew.